The New Boy from LA

誰是他爸爸？

Coleen Reddy　著

倪靖、郜欣、王平　繪

蘇秋華　譯

三民書局

For Thierry

   My Best Friend

獻給我的摯友—Thierry

Amy, David, and Jason were standing in front of Dogooder Junior High School before classes began. They were talking about computer games and comic books when they saw something strange.

1

They saw a limousine. It was shiny and black. It looked like it cost a million dollars. The limousine stopped in front of their school. The door opened and a boy stepped out. Everyone stared. The boy walked past Amy and her friends and went into the school building.

"Wow, I wonder who that is," said Amy.

"He's probably a snob. Did you see how he walked? He had his nose in the air," said Jason.

"You're just jealous because instead of looking at you, all the girls are looking at the new boy," said David.

David and Amy laughed.

"You guys don't know what you're talking about," said
Jason angrily as he walked off.

"What's wrong with him? I was only joking," said David.

"Maybe he drank some sour milk for breakfast," said Amy.

The bell rang and they went
to their first class.

Five minutes after their English class started, the principal, Mr. Stern, walked into the classroom. The new boy was with him.

"Good morning everyone," said Mr. Stern, "I would like you to meet Kyle Roberts. He is a new student from Los Angeles and he will be attending our school. Please make him feel welcome."

Mr. Stern left the room and Kyle sat down.

As soon as class was over, everyone walked over to Kyle to introduce themselves. The students surrounded him. He was going to be very popular.

"Look at them," said Jason, pointing to the students that were talking to Kyle. "They only want to be his friends because he is rich and has a limo."

"I'd like a ride in a limo," said David. "I'm going to introduce myself."

Amy and David introduced themselves to Kyle. He seemed really nice. They even sat with him during lunch.

The next day at school, everyone was talking about Kyle. It was "Kyle this" and "Kyle that." Kyle's father was a famous Hollywood director who had tons of money. Kyle lived in a mansion with fifteen bedrooms and seven bathrooms. His mansion had a huge pool with slides. Jason was jealous. He thought everyone liked Kyle only because he was rich. He did not want to be friends with Kyle. Kyle was a show-off and he was stuck-up. Amy and David didn't think so. They thought Kyle was great and friendly. They also said it was exciting to be the friend of a Hollywood director's son.

During lunch, Amy and David spoke to Kyle. They had a
lot of questions to ask him.

"Why did your family move to this boring old town?"
asked David.

"My father was bored with Hollywood. He wanted to move
to a quiet, peaceful town," said Kyle.

"Have you ever been on a movie set?" asked Amy.

"Sure, lots of times. I can visit the set of any movie because my dad is so famous," replied Kyle.

"Wow!" said David. "How many actors have you met?"

"Too many to count," boasted Kyle. "I've even been to their homes."

"Your life is so exciting; we have boring lives," said David.

"Can we visit your house to see what it's like?" asked Amy.

Kyle looked uncomfortable.

"My father doesn't like visitors because he is always busy," said Kyle, "but I'll ask him anyway."

"Thank you," said Amy.

The next day, everyone was disappointed. Kyle's father said that his friends couldn't visit him. Kyle looked sad. The only one who looked happy was Jason. Jason was sure that Kyle was lying. There was no mansion, no pool, and no slides. He would have to see for himself.

Jason finally convinced Amy and David to go with him. They found Kyle's address in the telephone book and walked to his house. It took them a long time to get there; it was on the other side of the town. The house was surrounded by a high wall so they couldn't see anything from outside.

They were all good climbers. They climbed over the wall and there it was.

It was everything that Kyle had described, except that it all looked even better.

"This is amazing!" said David. Amy just stared, with her mouth open, at the beautiful mansion.

"Are you satisfied?" asked David, "or do you still think that Kyle is an evil liar?"

"I'm sorry," said Jason, "I was jealous because Kyle is so popular."

19

Just then they heard a noise. Before they knew what was
going on, an angry man was standing in front of them.
"What are you doing in my garden?" he yelled.
"We're Kyle's friends. We wanted to visit him," David said.
They were scared.

"Oh, I'll take you to him," said the man.

"It's an honor to meet you. Kyle said you're a famous director," said Amy.

"Thank you," said the man. He didn't smile.

"Kyle is lucky to have a famous father," said Jason.

"What? Kyle is not my son. He's my chauffeur's son. His father drives my limo," said the man.

"You mean that Kyle doesn't live in this mansion?" asked Amy.

"No, Kyle lives in a small cottage behind the mansion with his father. I live in the mansion," said the man.

Amy, Jason, and David stared at one another. Kyle had lied to them. He wasn't the son of a rich, famous director. Instead, his father WORKED FOR a rich, famous director. His father was a chauffeur so he drove the limo. That's why Kyle had come to school in a limo!

The director took them to a small house behind the mansion and then he went away. Amy knocked on the door. Kyle opened it.

"Hey, what are you doing here? I told you my dad doesn't like visitors," said Kyle.

"You're lying. You didn't want us to visit because then we would know the truth. Your father is not a director and you're not rich," said Amy.

"We know everything," said David. "We met the REAL director."

25

Kyle looked very sad.

"You're right. I lied about everything," Kyle said quietly.

"Why did you lie to us?" asked Jason.

"I wanted to be popular. I was afraid of going to a new school because I didn't know anyone and I didn't have any friends," said Kyle.

"You don't have to be rich to have friends. We'll be your friends, but you have to be honest."

"Thanks a lot," said Kyle. "Do you guys want a ride in the limo? My dad's not busy now so he can drive us."

"YES!" screamed Amy, Jason, and David at the same time.

Kyle's father took them for a ride in the limo. The limo had a small TV and a little refrigerator with drinks in it. The most exciting part was that they could take the top off and stand up.

Amy, Jason, and David got their limo ride and Kyle got three real friends.

誰是他爸爸？

趁著還沒上課，愛玫、大維和杰生站在督顧德中學大門口討論電腦遊戲和漫畫書，就在這個時候，一件不尋常的事發生了：一輛看起來價值上百萬，黑得發亮的豪華大轎車在校門口停了下來。車門打開，一個男孩子走出來。所有的人都盯著他看，而男孩只是面無表情地走過愛玫和朋友面前，直接進了學校。

愛玫說：「哇，不曉得他是什麼人。」

杰生說：「八成是個勢利鬼，你看到他走路的樣子沒？好像鼻孔長在頭頂似的，一臉傲氣。」

大維說：「你只是嫉妒他罷了，因為女生都在看他，卻沒人看你。」說完，他和愛玫一起笑了。

杰生氣得甩頭就走，邊走還邊回嘴：「你們這些傢伙根本什麼都不懂。」

大維納悶地說：「他是怎麼搞的？我只不過是開開玩笑而已。」

愛玫說：「可能早上吃壞肚子了。」

上課鐘響了，他們進教室上第一堂課。

(p.1～p.5)

英文課開始不到五分鐘，嚴校長便走進教室，身旁還帶著新來的轉學生。

嚴校長說：「大家早，我想介紹凱爾‧羅伯茲給各位認識。他從洛杉磯轉來我們學校，請各位以後多多照顧他。」

嚴校長離開後，凱爾就到他的位置上坐下來。下課鐘才剛敲完，大家就一擁而上搶著向凱爾自我介紹。全部同學都環繞著他，看起來，凱爾會相當受歡迎。

杰生指著那些跟凱爾講話的同學，說：「你看他們，他們想跟他交朋友，就只是因為他家有錢，可以坐大轎車來上學。」

大維卻說：「我也想試試看坐大轎車是什麼滋味，那我也要去跟他自我介紹。」 愛玫和大維便一起去認識凱爾，他看起來人還不錯。吃中飯的時候，他們還跟他坐在一起。

第二天，學校裡上上下下都在討論凱爾的事，同學們開口閉口都是凱爾長，凱爾短。凱爾的爸爸是有名的好萊塢導演，鈔票多得數不完。凱爾住的是豪宅，裡面有十五間房間，七間浴室，還有一座巨型游泳池和溜滑梯。杰生很嫉妒，他認為大家喜歡凱爾，充其量只是因為他有錢。杰生才不屑跟凱爾做朋友呢！他覺得凱爾又愛現，又高傲。可是愛玫和大維卻不這麼認為。他們覺得凱爾很不錯，人又很好，他們還說，能跟好萊塢大導演的兒子交朋友真是令人興奮。

(p.7～p.11)

吃中飯的時候，愛玫和大維一直跟凱爾說話，他們有許多問題想問他。

大維問：「你們家為什麼要搬到這個無聊透頂的老鎮來？」

凱爾說：「因為我爸爸他過膩了好萊塢的生活，想搬到小鎮來讓耳根子靜一靜。」

愛玫問：「那你有沒有去片廠參觀過？」

凱爾回答：「當然有啦，去過很多次呢！因為我爸爸很有名，所以我想去哪個片廠，就可以去哪個片廠。」

大維很羨慕：「哇！那你看過哪些明星？」

凱爾大聲誇耀：「多得數不完，我還去過他們家喲！」

大維說：「你的生活真是多采多姿，哪像我們這麼乏味。」

（p.12～p.14）

愛玫說：「我們可不可以去你家玩，順便見識見識？」

這時凱爾的表情卻有點不自在。

他說：「我爸爸不喜歡有客人來，因為他太忙了。不過我還是可以問他
一下。」

愛玫很高興：「謝了。」

但是第二天，大家卻失望了。凱爾的爸爸不准他帶朋友回家。凱爾看起
來也很難過。當天唯一高興的人是杰生，他一口咬定凱爾在說謊，哪有
什麼豪宅、游泳池、溜滑梯。他還打算親自去探查一番。

（p.14～p.15）

杰生花了九牛二虎之力，總算說服愛玫和大維一起去「見識」凱爾的家。他們從電話簿裡查出凱爾家的地址，然後走路到他家。凱爾家位於小鎮的另一頭，因此他們走了很久才到。房屋的四周都用高聳的圍牆隔起來，從外頭沒辦法看出什麼名堂。好在他們三個都是爬牆高手，索性爬到牆上去一窺究竟。看到了！凱爾所言非但不假，而且看起來更高級，更奢華。

大維說：「真是太了不起了！」而愛玫只能張大嘴，猛盯著眼前華美的宅院。

大維對杰生說：「現在你滿意了吧？你不會再說凱爾是個大騙子了吧？」

杰生很不好意思地說：「對不起，我只是因為凱爾太受歡迎，所以嫉妒他罷了。」

就在這個時候，他們聽到一陣聲響，在還沒來得及反應之前，就看到一個氣呼呼的男人站在他們面前。

（p.16～p.20）

他大吼：「你們在我的庭院裡做什麼？」

大維說：「我們是凱爾的朋友，只是想來看看他而已。」他們三個人怕得要死。

那個人才平息下來，說：「好吧，我帶你們去找他。」

愛玫說：「很榮幸能見到你，凱爾說你是個很有名的導演。」

男人嘴上說了聲「謝謝」，可是臉上並沒有笑容。

杰生說：「凱爾真幸運，有你這麼有名的爸爸。」

男人一臉奇怪的表情：「你說什麼？凱爾才不是我兒子，他是我司機的兒子，他爸爸幫我開車。」

愛玫問：「你的意思是說，凱爾不住在這棟大房子裡？」

大導演回答：「不，大房子是我住，他跟他爸爸住在我家後面的小屋子裡。」

愛玫、杰生，和大維互相使了使眼色。凱爾騙了他們，他才不是什麼有錢大導演的兒子呢！他只是司機的兒子，而他爸爸幫有錢的大導演開車。這也就是為什麼凱爾可以坐大轎車來上學了。

（p.20～p.23）

大導演帶他們三個人繞到豪宅後面的一間小屋，然後就離開了。愛玫敲了敲門，開門的正是凱爾。

凱爾說：「咦？你們怎麼會在這裡？我不是跟你們說我爸爸不喜歡客人來的嗎？」

愛玫坦白地說：「你騙人。你不希望我們來玩是因為怕被我們知道你爸爸根本不是導演，而且你家也沒有錢。」

大維說：「我們什麼都知道了，剛才我們見過真正的導演了。」

凱爾看起來難過得不得了。

他低聲懺悔：「對啦，我騙了你們大家。」

杰生問：「你為什麼要這麼做？」

凱爾回答：「因為我希望自己受人歡迎。剛到一所新學校我好怕，我什麼人都不認識，而且連一個朋友也沒有。」

（p.24～p.27）

「你就算沒錢也交得到朋友啊，我們會當你的朋友，條件是你以後不可以再騙人了。」

凱爾很感激：「謝謝。你們想不想坐大轎車兜風呢？我爸爸現在有空，他可以載我們喔。」

愛玫、杰生和大維齊聲大喊：「太棒了！」

凱爾的爸爸用大轎車載他們兜風。車子裡有小電視，還有一個冰著冷飲的小冰箱。最棒的是，車頂可以打開，他們可以站起來吹風。愛玫、杰生和大維實現了坐大轎車的夢，而凱爾也交到了三個知心朋友。

（p.29～p.33）

全新的大喜故事來囉！這回大喜又將碰上什麼？讓我們趕快來瞧瞧！

Anna Fienberg & Barbara Fienberg／著　Kim Gamble／繪　柯美玲・王盟雄／譯

大喜與奇妙鐘

哎呀呀！
村裡的奇妙鐘被河盜偷走了，
聰明的大喜
能幫村民們取回奇妙鐘嗎？

大喜與大臭蟲

可惡的大巨人！
不但吃掉人家的烤豬，
還吃掉人家的兒子。
大喜有辦法將巨人趕走嗎？

大喜與魔笛

糟糕！走了一群蝗蟲，
卻來了個吹笛人，
把村裡的孩子們都帶走了。
快來瞧瞧大喜是怎麼救回他們的！

...樣的難題呢？

大喜與算命仙

大喜就要死翹翹了！？
這可不妙！
盧半仙提議的方法，
真的救得了大喜嗎？

大喜勇退惡魔

蜘蛛、蛇和老鼠！
惡魔們絞盡腦汁要逼大喜
說出公主的下落，
大喜要怎麼從惡魔手中逃脫呢？

大喜與寶鞋

大喜的表妹阿蓮失蹤了！
為了尋找阿蓮，
大喜穿上了飛天的寶鞋。
寶鞋究竟會帶他到哪裡去呢？

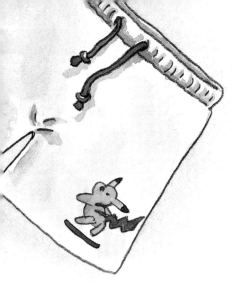

國家圖書館出版品預行編目資料

The New Boy from LA:誰是他爸爸？ / Coleen Reddy
著；倪靖, 郜欣, 王平繪；蘇秋華譯.－－初版一刷.
－－臺北市；三民，2002
面；公分--(愛閱雙語叢書. 青春記事簿系列)
中英對照
ISBN 957-14-3659-3　　(平裝)

805

© 　The New Boy from LA
　　──誰是他爸爸？

著作人　Coleen Reddy
繪　圖　倪靖　郜欣　王平
譯　者　蘇秋華
發行人　劉振強
著作財
產權人　三民書局股份有限公司
　　　　臺北市復興北路三八六號
發行所　三民書局股份有限公司
　　　　地址／臺北市復興北路三八六號
　　　　電話／二五○○六六○○
　　　　郵撥／○○○九九九八──五號
印刷所　三民書局股份有限公司
門市部　復北店／臺北市復興北路三八六號
　　　　重南店／臺北市重慶南路一段六十一號
初版一刷　西元二○○二年十一月
編　號　S 85620
定　價　新臺幣參佰伍拾元整
行政院新聞局登記證局版臺業字第○二○○號

ISBN　957-14-3659-3　　(平裝)

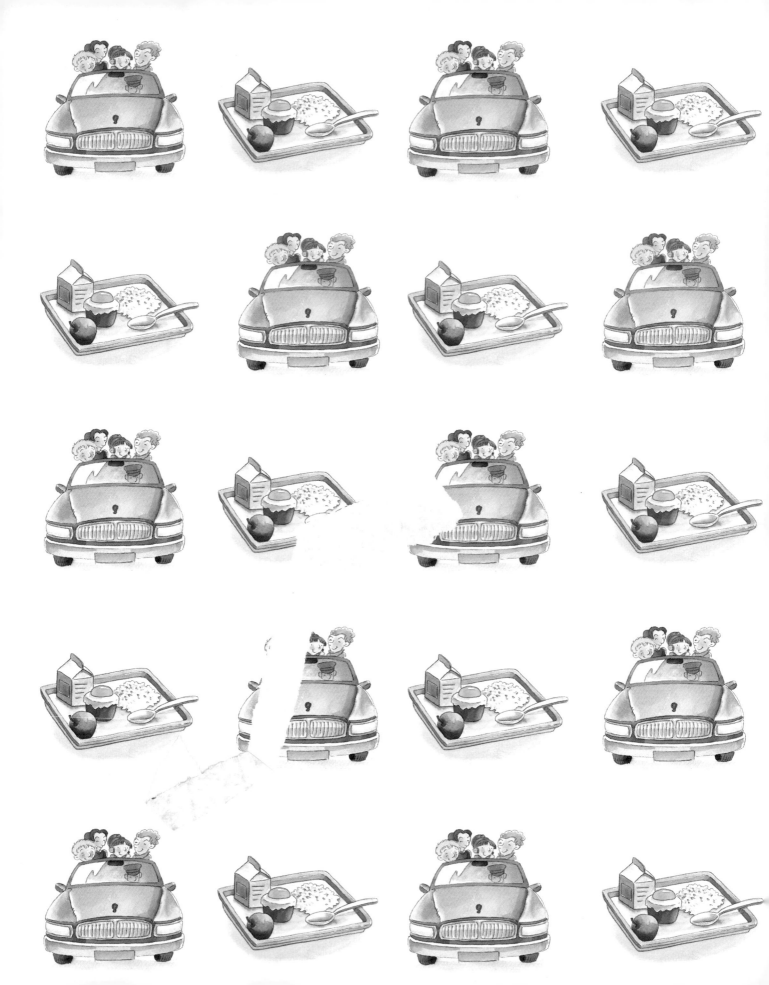